Library of Congress Cataloging-in-Publication Data Available

10 9 8 7 6 5 4 3 2 1

Published in 2004 by Sterling Publishing Co., Inc.
387 Park Avenue South, New York, NY 10016
Text copyright © 2003 Fernleigh Books
Illustration copyright © 2003 Daniel Howarth
Distributed in Canada by Sterling Publishing
c/o Canadian Manda Group, One Atlantic Avenue, Suite 105
Toronto, Ontario, Canada M6K 3E7

Sterling ISBN 1-4027-1625-7

The Chicken Who Saved Christmas

The Chicken Who Saved Christmas

Illustrated by Daniel Howarth

Sterling Publishing Co., Inc.
New York

It was Christmas Eve, and the morning sun shone into the hen house, waking Chicken and warming her feathers. "Time to get up!" she thought. "And what a day it's going to be! I love Christmas!" And she shook her feathers and strutted out into the farmyard.

There wasn't another soul around. The sleigh was muddy and empty, the harnesses hung unused on the wall, and Chicken could see the reindeer's heads nodding in the stable. They were fast asleep.

"What's going on?" thought Chicken. "Has everyone forgotten about Christmas?"

Chicken was worried, so she went off to find Santa.
But when she looked through his window,
there he was still in bed, looking very sorry for
himself, with watering eyes and a shiny red nose!
"Santa's ill!" thought Chicken. "Too ill to deliver the
Christmas presents! Disaster!" she clucked. "Calamity!!"
she squawked, and rushed off to tell the other animals.

"Reindeer, wake up!" squawked Chicken.
"What's all the fuss about?" yawned the chief reindeer.
"It's getting late," clucked Chicken, "and Santa's ill,
so please help me, or Christmas will be ruined!"
"We're so tired, and it's cold outside,"
said one reindeer snootily. "Go and ask the
other animals to help you."
So Chicken turned and ran to the big barn.

"Emergency, emergency!
All animals to the big barn immediately!"
Chicken squawked at the top of her voice. At once the silent farm
was alive with rustling and snuffling as the sleepy animals made
their way to the barn. Chicken explained what had happened.

"So it's up to us to make Christmas happen," she finished. "Who is with me?"

"We are," said the goats.

"And us," said the cats.

"And us," said all the others.

"Then let's get moving!" said Chicken.

The animals worked so hard to save Christmas!
The sheep polished the sleigh.
Horse and Pig loaded the presents.
The mice got the harnesses ready.
And Chicken squawked instructions
until her throat was sore!

"Good work!" she said when everything was ready.
"Now let's help Santa to get well."
And they ran off to Santa's house.

"Goat, help Santa to dress, please," said Chicken.
   "Right you are," said Goat.
Meanwhile, Duck stroked Santa's brow, Cat combed his hair,
and Cow gave him a warm drink of sweet fresh milk.

"Well done, everyone!!" said Santa. "And thank you, Chicken. You've saved the day!" and he patted Chicken on the head. "I'm feeling a little better, so I'd better set off," he added.

"Hurray!" all the animals cried as Santa climbed aboard.
But something was wrong . . . where were the reindeer?

Chicken rushed to the stable.
"No one is going anywhere on that sleigh today,
I'm afraid," said a reindeer sleepily. "You didn't remember
to feed us and it's too late now. We reindeer could never
fly on a full stomach!"

"Disaster!" shrieked all the animals, "Christmas is doomed!" and they started to run and hop and flap in panic. All except for Chicken. She was already devising another plan.

"ALRIGHT!" Chicken shouted. "Christmas WILL happen this year! WE will pull the sleigh! Farm animals, to your stations!" Cow was surprised and Pig was scared, but they knew better than to argue with Chicken!

To the reindeer's amazement, Santa's farm animals were harnessed up to the sleigh. Then Santa raised his hand, and shouted, "Candycane candies!" A shower of stars flew from his fingers onto his loyal animal friends.

Suddenly the horse, the goat, the cow, the sheep,
the pig and the cat could fly! They circled
the farm once, and flew off into the night.

And where was Chicken all this time?
Well, of course, she had the seat of honor
beside Santa. She puffed up her feathers
with pride and simply couldn't
stop herself smiling. Chicken
had saved Christmas!